for Ottoline

First published in Great Britain in 1997 by Andersen Press Ltd., 20 Vauxhall Bridge Road, London SW1V 2SA. Published in Australia by Random House Australia Pty., 20 Alfred Street, Milsons Point, Sydney, NSW 2061. Colour separated in Switzerland by Photolitho AG, Zürich. Printed and bound in Italy by Grafiche AZ, Verona.

10 9 8 7 6 5 4 3 2 1

British Library Cataloguing in Publication Data available.
ISBN 0 86264 747 9

This book has been printed on acid-free paper and is set in Goudy and Caslon Open-Face

Little Miss Muffet Counts to Ten

Emma Chichester Clark

A
Andersen Press • London

Little Miss Muffet
Sat on a tuffet,
Eating her curds and whey;
There came a big spider,
Who sat down beside her
And frightened Miss Muffet away.

Traditional nursery rhyme

1

Little Miss Muffet
Sat on a tuffet,
Eating her curds and whey,
When along came one spider
Who sat down beside her,
And said to Miss Muffet,
"Please stay!"

Little Miss Muffet
Sat on the tuffet,
Eating her curds and whey,
When along came two Lemurs
With trumpets and streamers,
And bunting to make a display.

2

3

Little Miss Muffet
Sat on the tuffet,
Eating her curds and whey,
When along came three magpies
With taffeta bow-ties,
And waistcoats of very pale grey.

Little Miss Muffet
Sat on the tuffet,
Eating her curds and whey,
When along came four foxes
With neatly wrapped boxes,
And jellies lined up on a sleigh.

4

Little Miss Muffet
Sat on the tuffet,
Eating her curds and whey,
When along came five pussycats
With milkshake and party hats,
And small pots of chocolate soufflé.

5

6

Little Miss Muffet
Sat on the tuffet,
Eating her curds and whey,
When along came six poodles
With oodles of noodles,
And flutes which they started to play.

Little Miss Muffet
Sat on the tuffet,
Eating her curds and whey,
When along came seven bears
With a table and chairs.
They said, “We’ll sit here, if we may.”

7

Little Miss Muffet
Sat on the tuffet,
Eating her curds and whey,
When along came eight puffins
With blueberry muffins,
And each clutched a tiny bouquet.

8

Little Miss Muffet
Sat on the tuffet,
Eating her curds and whey,
When along came nine gibbons
With balloons tied with ribbons,
And bananas arranged on a tray.

9

10

Little Miss Muffet
Sat on the tuffet,
Eating her curds and whey,
When along came ten crocodiles
With a box and ten greedy smiles.
They saw her and shouted, "HOORAY!"

Little Miss Muffet
Jumped up from her tuffet;
She looked at the box in dismay.
Were they taking her back
In a box as a snack?
But she waited to hear what they'd say.
AND...

There was cheering and prancing,
And whooping and dancing -
And what did the crocodiles say?
"You have made a mistake;
We have brought you a cake!
Don't you know? It's your birthday today!"

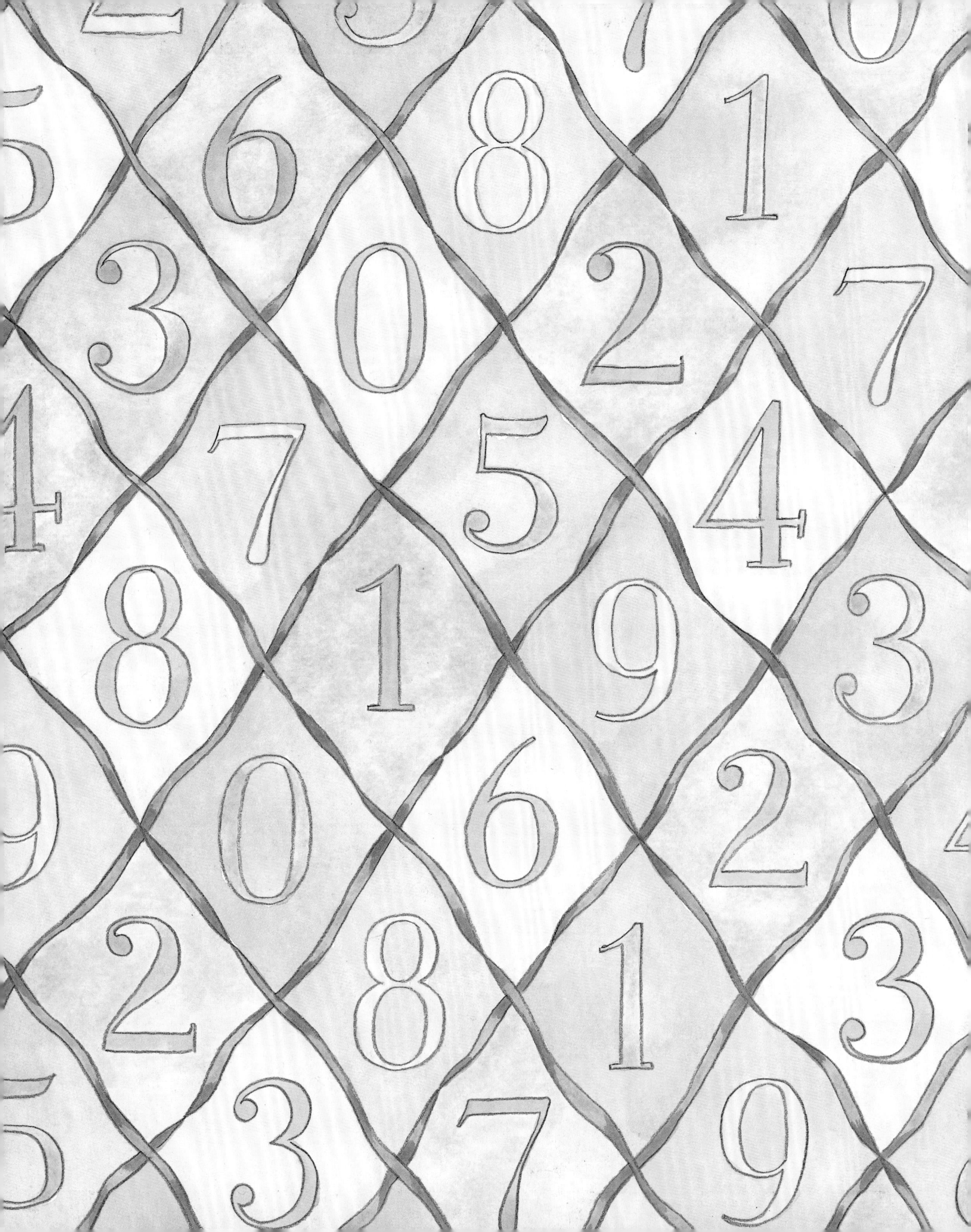